FREMONT PUBLIC LIBRARY
3 3090 00635 2704
W9-BAH-643
3-21

For Ben and Frankie,
paddling on the other side
of the globe

Copyright © 2019 by Sebastien Braun

All rights reserved. No part of this book may be reproduced, transmitted, or stored in an information retrieval system in any form or by any means, graphic, electronic, or mechanical, including photocopying, taping, and recording, without prior written permission from the publisher.

First US edition 2021
First published by Templar Books, an imprint of Bonnier Books UK, 2019

Library of Congress Catalog Card Number pending
ISBN 978-1-5362-1705-6

20 21 22 23 24 25 TLF 10 9 8 7 6 5 4 3 2 1

Printed in Dongguan, Guangdong, China

This book was typeset in Providence Sans.
The illustrations were created digitally.

TEMPLAR BOOKS
an imprint of
Candlewick Press
99 Dover Street
Somerville, Massachusetts 02144

www.candlewick.com

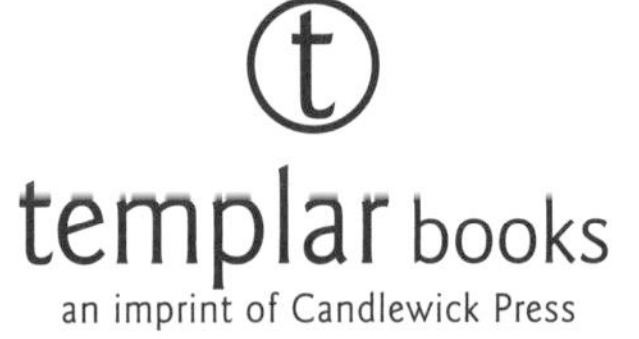

Raj and the BEST VACATION EVER!

WITHDRAWN
FREMONT PUBLIC LIBRARY DISTRICT
1170 N. Midlothian Road
Mundelein, IL 60060

Sebastien Braun

Dad and I are going on a trip today.
I know it's going to be the
BEST VACATION EVER!

Dad is getting everything ready.
There is so much to put
in the car!

Are we going
to Antarctica?

"Not that far, Raj," says Dad. "We're going camping."

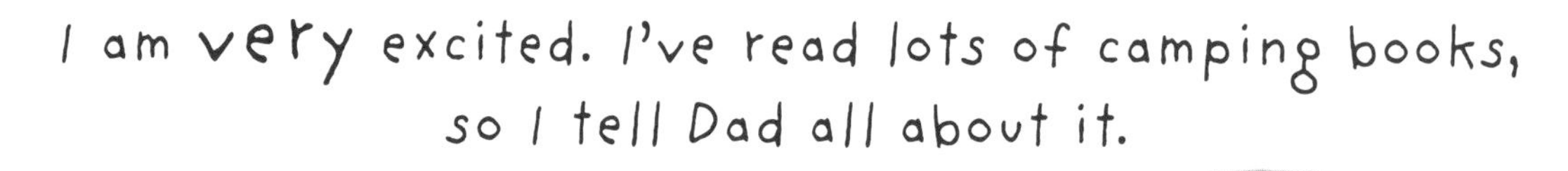
I am very excited. I've read lots of camping books,
so I tell Dad all about it.

You need a tent to sleep in . . .
sleeping bag
R4J 1
and a stove to cook on.
R4J 1
sleeping bag

You also need hiking boots to climb big mountains!

R4J1

And best of all, you can go in a canoe!

You know a lot more about this than I do, Raj!

R4J1

When the car is packed,
we set off!
SUPERMARKET
We play the
I Spy game.
I spy
something
beginning
with T!
We sing our
favorite
songs.
The wheels
on the bus
go round and
round.
Are we
there yet?
I ask helpful
questions.
Are we
there yet?
CAMPSITE

After a while, Dad stops
at a gas station.
I need to stop, too!

I don't know how
Dad knows where to go,
but he does.

And after a really long time . . .

We arrive at the campsite. It's beautiful!
"This is going to be the best vacation EVER!"
I say.

Dad finds a space for
our little tent beside a
HUMONGOUS one.

I hold the flashlight so Dad can put up the tent.

It seems to be taking a long time . . .

but when the family of bears in the
humongous tent next door offers to help . . .

Dad says, "No, thank you."
Finally, he hammers in the last stake!

When we get in our sleeping bags, I realize that I need to go to the bathroom. I tell Dad, but he doesn't say anything, so I tell him again.

Dad, I really, really, really, REALLY need to go!

I tell him until he gets up to take me.

It's dark, and on the way, Dad trips over something.

When we wake up in the morning, I am **very** excited.
Dad says it's too early to be so excited,
but I don't agree.

We're going to cook on our **camp stove!**

But things don't go quite the way Dad planned.

The family of bears invites us to join them for breakfast, but Dad says, “No, thank you.”

We eat cereal instead.

After breakfast, Dad says, "Let's go for a hike!"

So we do!

Can you see the top of the mountain, Raj? That's where we are going!

That's far, far, far away!

SHORT ROUTE

LONG ROUTE

There is
so much
to see!

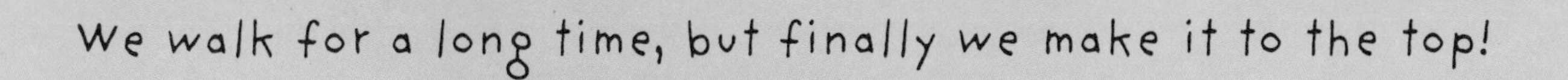
We walk for a long time, but finally we make it to the top!

Then we hear . . .

♫
SHE'LL BE
COMING ROUND THE
MOUNTAIN WHEN
SHE COMES . . .
♪♪

The bears from the campsite arrive!
I ask Dad if we can join in their song,
but he doesn't say anything.
Aye, aye
yippee yippee . . .
aye, aye
yippee
yippee . . .
AYE!!
Sing it!
"Can we go back to the tent now?" I ask.

The bears invite us to take the shortcut back with them,

but Dad says, "No, thank you," and we go back the way we came.

Walking down the mountain takes a long, long time.

Dad says it isn't far, but it seems like it is.

Soon, I am really thirsty, so Dad takes out the bottle . . .

There is no water left in our bottle.

"This is the

WORST VACATION EVER!"

I tell Dad.

"We're almost back to the campsite," says Dad.

"And after lunch, I have a special surprise."

It's a GREAT surprise!

See, Dad? I KNEW we would go canoeing if we went camping!

I tell Dad that I know just the song
for a surprise like this, and we sing it.

Dad is enjoying singing so much

that he doesn't see something important.

Our **paddle is lost,** and we missed the turn!

We are going down the river fast, and there's a drop-off ahead!

Just then, we see the family of bears.

The mommy and daddy bears ask Dad if he needs help.

This time Dad says, "YES, thank you!"

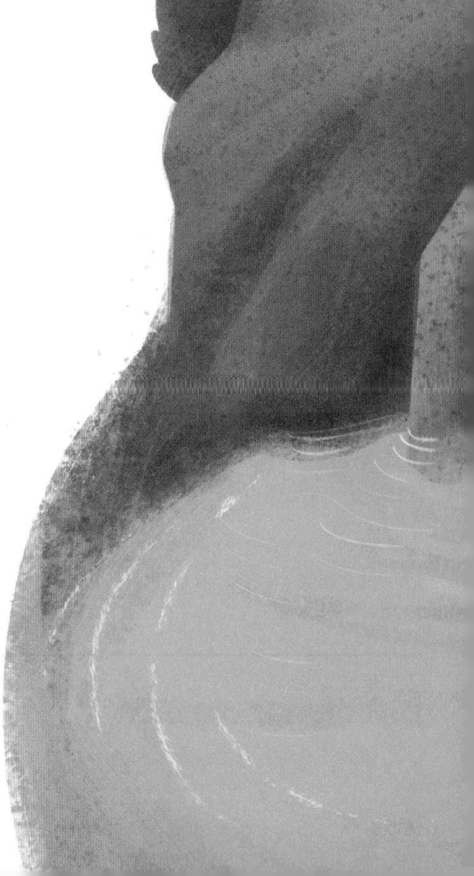

The bear family
does something
AMAZING!

And we are saved.
Just like that!

Then the littlest bear
asks us a question.

And I say,
"YES, THANK YOU!"

We have so much fun that I ask Dad
if we can go camping again next year.

He says yes.

And then I tell him,

"This is
definitely the
BEST VACATION
EVER!"

The end!